The Moon City

Written by Rebecca Clements

Illustrated by Gloria Vanessa Nicoli

Written by Rebecca Clements

Text copyright Rebecca Clements ©2020

Illustrated by Gloria Vanessa Nicoli

Illustrations Copyright Rebecca Clements ©2020 First

Edition 2020

The Moon City

ISBN : 978-1-8382938-0-2

To,
Isabella & William,

I love you to the moon city and back again.

As the sun slowly set and darkness descended like a heavy blanket on sleepy London, the Penny Mice family got to work.

For centuries, their family have lived and worked on the moon. Mr. and Mrs. Penny and their 15 children had the very important job of lighting up the world with the moon when the sun went to bed each evening.

You see, the world needed a light at night. It helped soothe children who were afraid of the dark, guided night-time animals like hedgehogs and owls to find food and shelter and provided a very important service to the tooth fairy and other magical creatures.

*E*ach evening, the Penny mice would run on giant wheels that powered the moon to light up brightly in the sky. And from it they could gaze in amazement at the wonderful world below. They saw all sorts of things from the sky. Bedtime stories being read, children sleepily sipping warm milk by fireplaces, foxes playing with old balls in residential streets and cats stealthily hunting mice.

*I*t was a cold day in winter, and Mr. and Mrs. Penny sat huddled whispering urgently to one another. A storm was brewing over London, and reports said it was going to be the worst storm in the history of storms.

Giant black and heavy rainclouds filled the sky, and a howling wind whooshed around London, leaving a trail of damp leaves, mud and broken umbrellas. Children wrapped up warm in scarfs and hats were shuffled home as quickly as possible by parents eager for nobody to catch a cold.

"*T*he sun will be setting soon; these clouds are the worst I've ever seen," Mr. Penny anxiously said as he peered at London below. "How ever will we light up the city tonight?"

"We won't even be able to blow these clouds out of the way with our blowing machine, Pa... they are too heavy and filled with rain," Mrs. Penny replied, pacing in front of the fire.

Mr. and Mrs. Penny decided to call an urgent meeting with the children. Darkness was only an hour away, and they had never let the world down before. They had to find a solution, and quickly!

Gathered around the dining table as thunder and lightning filled the room with low rumbles and bright flashes, the family tried to figure out a plan but were getting nowhere. The storm really was the very worst they had ever seen, and they all felt so sad and deflated. How scary for the children below this must be - they must have light tonight.

*"L*et's eat some cheese. That always helps me think harder," said the youngest of the Penny Mice, Kimberley, as she took a huge chunk and squidged it in her mouth.

"OH, MY GOODNESS, THAT'S IT!" shouted Alexander, the oldest of the Penny mice children, suddenly making everyone jump.

"If we can't get the moon to be bright enough from the sky, let's take the moon to London."

Kimberley opened her mouth in disbelief and cheese fell out everywhere. Spluttering, she said, "Have you lost your cheese grater? How on earth are we going to do that?"

"No... it could work" Mr. Penny interrupted. "I think I might have a plan. Listen close," he said as the group huddled in, eager to get going.

*W*ith half hour until nightfall, the Penny mice children were busy biting off chunks of the moon (which luckily, in case you didn't know, is made of cheese). Once they'd taken a chunk, they stuffed it in rucksacks until they could squeeze no more in. Next up, it was time to parachute to London.

With a huge leap, all the Penny mice took a giant jump off the moon, which had a big hole in the side of it, and parachuted to London.

"WEEEEEEEEEEEE!" shouted Kimberley who was holding two extra lumps of cheese in each hand, in case she got hungry on the journey.

A rriving, in the wet, windy and miserable city, they got to work straight away. Time was ticking. Alexander and Mr. Penny's great plan was indeed genius. Scuttering around London, they filled all the streetlamps with pieces of the moon. Soon, the streets were ablaze with bright lights, making the harsh cold day somewhat cosy and warm looking.

As the darkness set in and the sun went to bed, the Penny children filled the last few streetlamps and dashed back home on a kite that was a victim to the storm.

*F*rom the moon that evening, they gazed at the shimmering city of London below. Though the storm was still going, the city was alight, and everyone was tucked up in beds comfy and warm. The plan had been a success.

The Penny family still live on the moon today, in Moon City, where each night they work hard to power the moon to fill the world with light. However, if you ever look up and see it with a bit missing, it's probably because a city somewhere has a storm and the mice had to go and fill streetlamps with cheese. Don't panic, they will make more cheese and the moon will be whole again in a few short days.

THE END

Printed in Great Britain
by Amazon